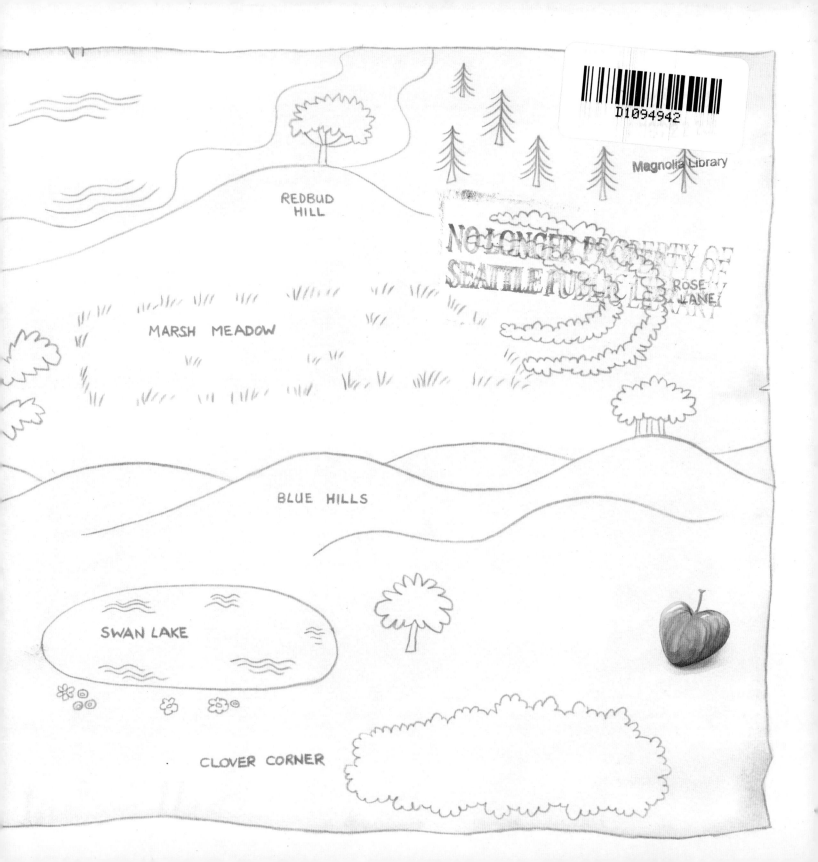

REDBUD HILL

MARSH MEADOW

ROSE LANE

BLUE HILLS

SWAN LAKE

CLOVER CORNER

For Charlotte, Wes, and Vera
—C.G.

For my lovely Nan who sends me hearts to guide my path
—J.E.

Little Hearts
Text copyright © 2022 Charles Ghigna • Illustrations copyright © Jacqueline East
First published in 2022 by Red Comet Press LLC, Brooklyn, NY
Library of Congress Control Number: 2022930005
ISBN (HB): 978-1-63655-030-5 • ISBN (EBOOK): 978-1-63655-031-2
22 23 24 25 TLF 10 9 8 7 6 5 4 3 2 1
First Edition • Manufactured in China

RedCometPress.com

Little Hearts

Written by **CHARLES GHIGNA**

Illustrations by **JACQUELINE EAST**

RED COMET PRESS · BROOKLYN

The world is full of little hearts.
Each one a sign of love.

Some are found upon the ground.

Some are up above.

Little seashells on the shore.
Some look like a heart!

Each leaf upon the redbud tree
Looks like a work of art!

The smell of roses in the air.
They blossom in the sun.

Each petal is a little heart.
A very fragrant one.

Puffy clouds go drifting by.
Oh, what a dreamy sight!

One looks like a Valentine—
A fluffy heart of white.

The busy spider spins her web.
She keeps a steady pace.

She weaves a silky gift of love—
A little heart of lace.

A farmer's field of strawberries.
We pick a few to eat.

Red hearts growing in a row.
Each one a tasty treat!

An apple tree upon the hill.
What a sweet surprise.

When you slice one open—
Two hearts before your eyes!

Walnuts scattered on the ground.
Some are open wide.

Who knew that in a big brown nut
A little heart would hide?

A bashful little ladybug
Hiding in a tree.

She wears a polka-dotted heart
And brings good luck to me.

See the swans out on the lake
Swimming in the sun.

Two of them together make
A little heart of one.

Walking through
a clover patch

Green hearts
everywhere.

We find a lucky
four-leaf one.

A treasure we
can share.

A sweet bouquet of butterflies.
We wave as they depart.

They fly away on wings of love.
Each one a little heart.

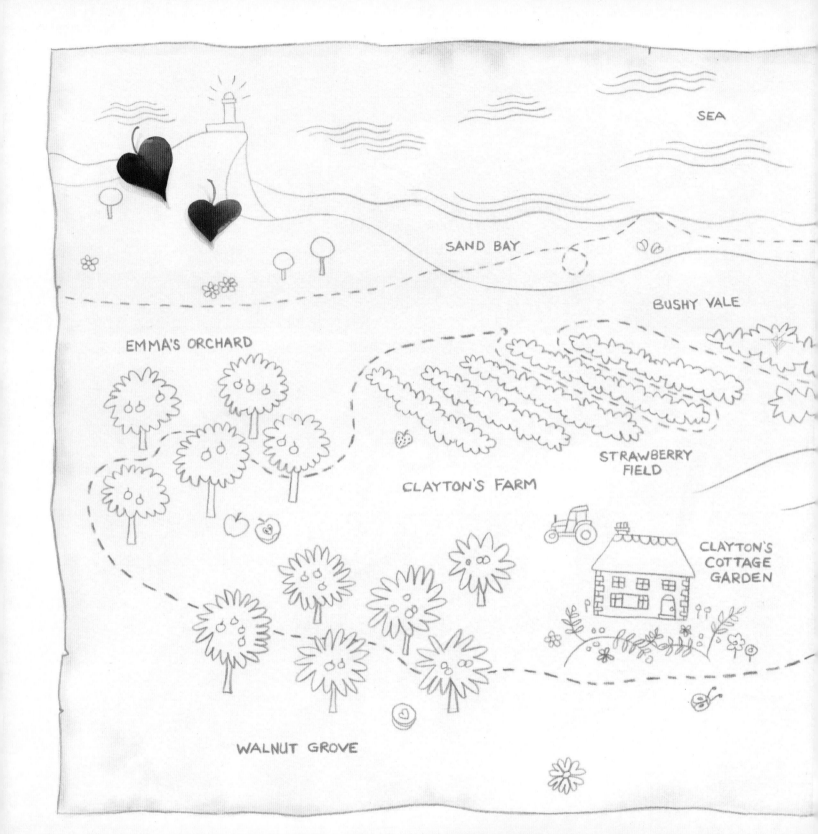